Our Lunch Boxes

By Anne Giulieri

It is lunchtime at school.
We are all hungry.
It is time to eat lunch.

We look inside our school bags.

Look at all the lunch boxes!

Look inside my lunch box.

In my lunch box, I see:

- a sandwich,
- an apple,
- and a drink.

Look inside my lunch box.

In my lunch box, I see:

- some cheese and crackers,

- some raisins,
- and a drink.

GOLDEN
RAISINS

Look inside my lunch box.

In my lunch box, I see:

- a cheese sandwich,

- crackers and dip,
- an orange,

- and a drink.

Look inside my lunch box.

In my lunch box, I see:

- a sandwich,
- a banana,
- and a drink.

Where is my lunch box?
Where is my lunch?

Look inside my lunch box.

I have a big lunch.
You can have some of my lunch.

Look!

We are all eating lunch.

We are all very hungry!